MUSIC for the TSAR of the SEA

A RUSSIAN WONDER TALE RETOLD BY

CELIA BARKER LOTTRIDGE

PICTURES BY

HARVEY CHAN

A GROUNDWOOD BOOK

Douglas & McIntyre   Toronto Vancouver Buffalo

LONG ago in the city of Novgorod there lived a young man called Sadko who was poor in everything but music. For Sadko's father had died leaving him nothing but an old *gusli*, a little harp made of maple wood. Sadko learned to play upon the *gusli* so well that he was called Sadko the minstrel.

The rich merchants of Novgorod were glad to have Sadko play at their feasts, and they were generous with the copper *kopeks* they threw into his hat. Sadko sang of the Russian forests and lakes that surrounded Novgorod, but he never sang of rivers or the sea. For Novgorod had no river, and the sea was far away. The copper *kopeks* did not make Sadko rich, but every day he earned enough to put bread in his belly, and he had his *gusli* and its music for company when he was lonely.

Then came a day when Sadko was not asked to play at a feast. As evening fell he decided to welcome the holiday. So he took his *gusli* and went to the shores of beautiful Lake Ilmen, which lies outside the walls of Novgorod. He sat on a rock and watched the moon rise and sang a song about the lake in the moonlight. As he sang, the waters of the lake began to swirl and rise until waves crashed upon the shore.

Sadko put his *gusli* under his shirt to protect it from wind and water and hurried back to the safety of the walls of Novgorod.

The next day, once again there was no feast, and Sadko returned to the rock beside the lake. The waters were calm, and he played a song about the gentle wind in the reeds. But then the wind rose and waves beat against the rock where Sadko sat. So once again he ran back through the gates of the city.

For the third day no one asked Sadko to play. He had only a few *kopeks* left to buy bread and nothing to sell but his *gusli*. "And I can't sell that," he said to himself, "for I am a minstrel." He thought about the lake and the strange waves that came only when he played. Then he picked up his little harp and went back to the rock on the shore.

This time he played the songs he would play for a wedding, for dancing and merrymaking. When the water began to swirl, Sadko didn't move. He played faster and faster and a great whirlpool formed in the middle of the lake.

Out of the whirlpool rose a giant of a man. His eyes were stormy gray, his flowing hair was green, and he wore a crown upon his head. Sadko stared in wonder. Then suddenly he knew. This was the Tsar of the Sea, ruler of oceans and seas, of lakes and rivers and all realms that lie under the water.

The Tsar of the Sea walked toward Sadko, churning up the water along the path of moonlight. When he was so near that Sadko could see silver drops of water shining in his long green beard, he stopped.

"Sadko of Novgorod," he said, and his voice was like the sound of waves breaking against a distant shore. "For three nights I have held a feast beneath the waters of Lake Ilmen, and I and my daughters and all of our guests have danced to the music you have played."

Sadko could not speak, but he bowed his head to show that he was honored.

"I wish to thank you for your music. Cast a net into these waters and whatever comes into it is my gift to you. And promise me that you will come to my palace under the sea and play for me there."

Sadko nodded because he still could not find his voice. Then the Tsar turned and walked back along the path of moonlight to the middle of the lake. The great waves of the whirlpool rose around him, and he sank beneath the waters. The surface of the lake calmed, and the path of moonlight lay still.

"Was it a dream?" said Sadko to himself. "It will do no harm to see." He found a net the fishermen had left near their boats and cast it into the lake. Then he sat down and made up a new song about the wonders that might lie beneath the water.

When the song had ended, he drew in the net. At first he thought it was empty, but in the last fold he found a small wooden chest bound in brass. It was filled with jewels—rubies as red as blood, sapphires as blue as the summer sky, and pearls glowing like little moons. Sadko lifted them and let them fall from his hands in a shining stream. Then he closed the chest and carried it into the city.

The next day he sold two jewels and bought a stall in the marketplace. From then on he was known as Sadko the merchant, not Sadko the minstrel. He played no more at feasts but traveled the rough roads from one end of Russia to the other seeking fine goods. When he needed money, he would sell a ruby or a sapphire from the little chest.

People forgot that Sadko had ever been a poor minstrel. They invited him to every feast and celebration in Novgorod. But Sadko had had enough of feasts when he sang for *kopeks*. In the rare times when he was not trading or traveling, he took his *gusli* out to the rock by the lake and sang old songs. And once he threw into the lake a necklace made of carved lapis lazuli, as blue as the water in summer. "This is for you, Tsar of the Sea," said Sadko, "in thanks for the gift you gave to me."

Twelve years passed. Now Sadko sailed the seas to trade in lands far from Russia. One summer day he sat on the deck of his own fine ship, playing his *gusli* softly so that only he could hear. Suddenly, the ship stopped. With its course set for a far port and its sails filled with wind, it stopped, right in the middle of the Caspian Sea.

The captain said, "We've gone aground. Take soundings." The sailors did, and the sea was forty fathoms deep at the bow and forty at the stern.

"Unless there's a spike of rock like a needle rising from the bottom of the sea, we are not aground," said the captain. "Put on more sails."

The sailors put on all the sails. The masts groaned and bent but the ship did not move. The men began to look at each other with frightened eyes. "The Tsar of the Sea wants something from us," they said.

"Give him a keg of gold," said Sadko. And the sailors threw a keg filled with gold coins into the sea. But the ship did not move. They threw in silver and then pearls, but the ship was motionless, as if it was held by a giant hand.

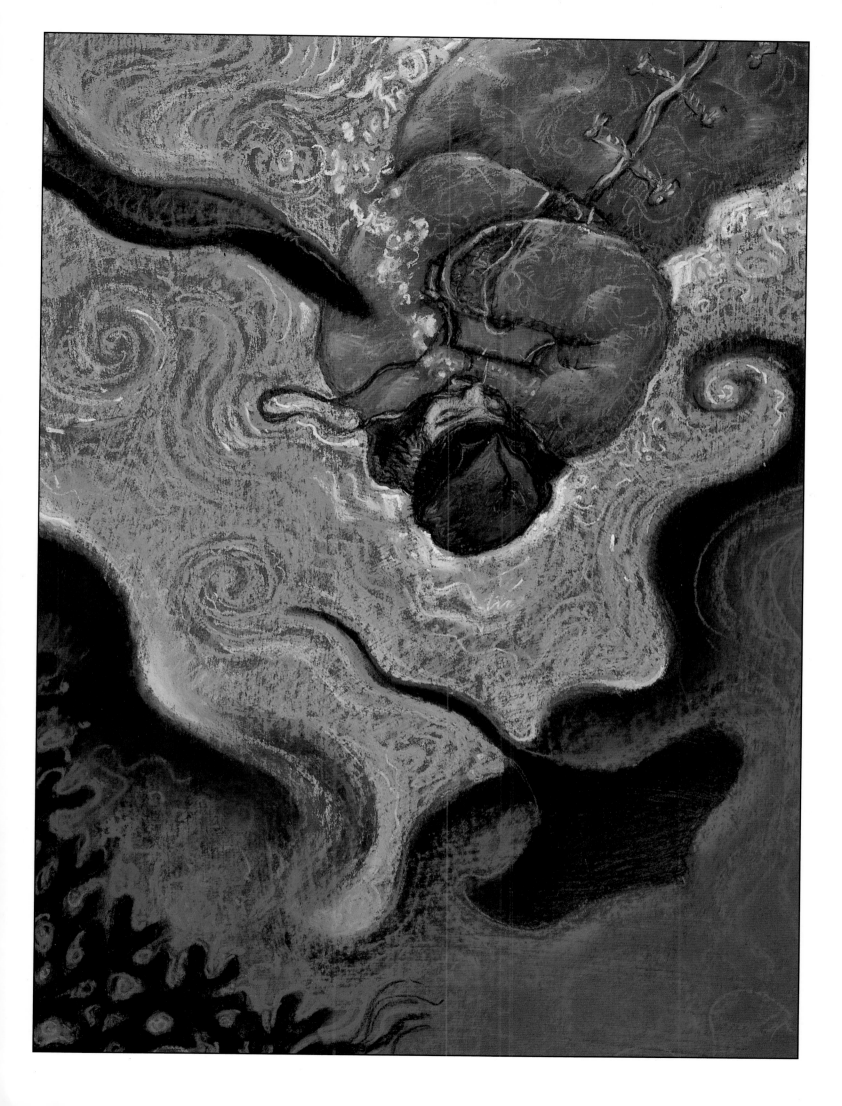

At last he stood on the bottom of the Caspian Sea. Before him rose the palace of the Tsar of the Sea, made of coral and timbers from sunken ships. Brightly colored fish swam in and out of the windows, and the great doorway was made of the jawbones of whales.

Sadko grasped his *gusli* firmly and walked through that doorway and into the great hall of the Tsar of the Sea. The Tsar was sitting on a throne decorated with shimmering shells. His green beard waved gently in the water.

When the Tsar saw Sadko his voice rumbled like stones shifting in a strong tide. "Sadko of Novgorod," he said, "my daughters and I have waited long to hear your music in our palace under the sea."

Now Sadko saw that on either side of the Tsar were seated young women with cloudy hair and gray eyes. "Great Tsar," said Sadko, "I am sorry I did not come to you sooner. But now I am here and I will play, if that is your wish."

"Play, then," said the Tsar.

First Sadko played old songs about Lake Ilmen. Then new ones about rivers and the sea seemed to flow from his fingers like water. The Tsar listened and smiled, but after a time, he rose from his throne.

"I will dance," he said. He walked through the great doorway, out onto the sandy bottom of the sea.

Then Sadko played and the Tsar of the Sea danced. As he danced he grew until his green beard looked to Sadko like seaweed floating far above. The waters began to move with the dance. Up on the surface of the sea, waves crashed against the shore, ships were tossed about, wharves were swept away and towns were flooded.

Sadko could feel the great storm above him, but if he stopped playing even for a moment, a thundering voice boomed, "Play faster. Do not stop."

Then he felt a touch on his shoulder. He turned, still play-ing, and saw one of the daughters of the Tsar. She spoke to him in a low voice. "Sadko, my father's dancing will bring great destruction to the ships and cities of the Caspian Sea. He will not stop while the music plays, and he will never want you to stop playing."

"What can I do?" said Sadko.

"Break the strings of your *gusli* and tell my father that you must return to Novgorod for new ones. He will let you go, but only if you take one of his daughters with you. Ask for me and all will be well. My name is Volkova."

As she turned to go into the palace, Sadko saw that around her neck she wore a necklace of carved lapis lazuli. But he was still playing and the storm raged, so he laid his fingers across the strings to silence them. Then one by one he broke each string.

The Tsar of the Sea stopped dancing, and the waters calmed. When Sadko did not answer his call, he shrank down to his usual enormous size. "Why did you stop playing?" he demanded.

"Oh, great Tsar," said Sadko. "The strings of my *gusli* are broken. I must return to Novgorod for new ones."

"You may go to Novgorod," said the Tsar. "But you must return so that I can dance again. Choose one of my daughters to go with you. She will bring you back to me."

Then all the daughters of the Tsar of the Sea came and stood before the palace. Sadko looked at one and then another until he saw one who wore a necklace of blue stones around her neck. Then he said, "This is the one I choose."

"That is Volkova," said the Tsar of the Sea. "Go with her."

Volkova led Sadko to a little room and said, "You must rest here. Then we will go together to Novgorod. Sadko, I have loved your songs since you played for our feast in Lake Ilmen. I hope you will always play for me. Yet it is not under the sea that you should play, but in the bright world above." Sadko thought about her words, but he was tired, and he fell asleep.

When he woke he was not in the palace of the Tsar of the Sea. The blue sky was above him. He turned his head and saw that he was lying outside the walls of Novgorod. And beside him flowed a river, a river he had never seen before.

He rose and walked to the edge of the river. It was broad and deep and flowed as if it had always been there. Sadko looked into the clear water and saw a flash of blue. It was a necklace of carved lapis lazuli.

And so the city of Novgorod got its river, the great river Volkov that flows to the Volga and on to the Caspian Sea. For the daughter of the Tsar of the Sea never returned to her father's palace.

And Sadko never went again to the Caspian Sea. Instead his ship sailed up and down the river Volkov while Sadko, a merchant and a minstrel, sat on the deck playing his *gusli*. And when the Tsar of the Sea danced, he danced gently to music far away, the music Sadko played for the river that loved his songs.